SESAME STREET

ELMO LOVES YOU

A Poem By Elmo

Elmo hopes you love his poem!

By Sarah Albee
Illustrated by Maggie Swanson

A GOLDEN BOOK • NEW YORK

"Sesame Workshop,"® "Sesame Street,"® and associated characters, trademarks, and design elements are owned and licensed by Sesame Workshop. Copyright © 1997, 2014 Sesame Workshop. All Rights Reserved. Published in the United States by Golden Books, an imprint of Random House Children's Books, a division of Random House LLC, a Penguin Random House Company, 1745 Broadway, New York, NY 10019, and in Canada by Random House of Canada Limited, Toronto, in conjunction with Sesame Workshop. Originally published by Golden Books, an imprint of Random House Children's Books, New York in 1997. Golden Books, A Golden Book, A Little Golden Book, the G colophon, and the distinctive gold spine are registered trademarks of Random House LLC.

Visit us on the Web!
randomhouse.com/kids
SesameStreetBooks.com
www.sesamestreet.org

ISBN: 978-0-385-37283-1

Printed in the United States of America
10 9 8 7 6 5 4

Random House Children's Books supports the First Amendment and celebrates the right to read.

Everyone loves something.
Babies love noise.
Birds love singing.

Kids love toys!

Bert loves pigeons, and pigeons love to coo.
Can you guess who Elmo loves? Elmo loves *you*!

Piggies love to roll in mud.

Penguins love the snow.

Farmers love to wake up early.
Roosters love to crow.

Zoe loves the library.
Grover loves it, too.
Elmo whispers quietly,
"Elmo loves *you*!"

The Count loves counting things.

Ernie loves to drum.

Monsters love to exercise.

Kids love bubble gum.

Natasha and her daddy love playing
  peekaboo.
But, *pssssst!*—before you turn the
  page—Elmo loves *you*!

Monkeys love bananas.

Kids love school.

Grouches love trash.

Big Bird loves the pool.

Everyone loves something.
Elmo told you this was true.
And now you know who Elmo loves:
Elmo loves *you*!

Before he ends his poem, Elmo wants
    to ask you this:
Will you be Elmo's valentine?
Could Elmo have a kiss?